For Marion from the beginning
And to Lydia for inspiration
halfway through — C B L

For my parents — P Z

The publisher gratefully acknowledges the
assistance of the Ontario Arts Council, the Canada
Council and the Ontario Ministry of Culture,
Tourism and Recreation.

Canadian Cataloguing in Publication Data

Lottridge, Celia B. (Celia Barker)
Something might be hiding

ISBN 0-88899-176-2

I. Zwolak, Paul.   II. Title.

PS8573.O855S6 1994   jC813'.54   C94-930083-7
PZ7.L67So 1994

A Groundwood Book
Douglas & McIntyre
585 Bloor Street West
Toronto, Ontario M6G 1K5

The illustrations are done in acrylic paint on canvas

Set in Adobe Garamond by Compeer Typographic Services
Design by Michael Solomon
Photography by See Spot Run, Toronto
Printed and bound in Hong Kong
by Everbest Printing Co. Ltd.

Something
Might
Be Hiding

By Celia Barker Lottridge
Pictures by Paul Zwolak

A Groundwood Book
Douglas & McIntyre
Toronto   Vancouver   Buffalo

NOTHING in the new house looked ordinary. The ironing board was on top of the piano, the sofa was facing the wall, and there were boxes everywhere.

Jenny walked around and around looking at all the
odd corners and upside-down furniture.

"Your room is at the top of the stairs," said her
mother.
Jenny went to look.

The room was clean and empty. It had a shiny floor
of golden wood.

Jenny went down to find her family. She walked past
the space under the stairs. It was crowded with boxes and
hockey sticks and lamps. Was there something behind
them? Jenny couldn't quite see.

"I think there is something hiding under the stairs,"
she told her mother. "Something big and furry. It might
be a bear but it makes a more muttering sound."

"Did you hear it?" said her mother.

"I'm almost sure," said Jenny.

"Let's move these boxes," said her mother. "We'll take them to the attic tomorrow. Then there will be no hiding place. And, see? There's nothing there."

Jenny looked. There was nothing there.

Jenny liked her room with her bed in it, all made up with her blue quilt. Her toys were still stacked, higgledy-piggledy, everywhere. Jenny shoved most of them into the closet.

The closet had a slanted ceiling and a low corner
at the back.

When Jenny needed to find her second-best teddy
bear among the toys, she noticed that corner.

"Something might be hiding there," she said to her father.

"Something with sharp, sharp teeth. But's it's very shy and it hates the light."

"Well," said her father. "There are a few things that don't really need to be in this closet. Let's put your doll house over here and these blocks under the window. There, now there's too much light. It will have to go away for sure."

Jenny opened the closet door. There was nothing in the corner but a stray patch of sunlight.

Jenny went to bed in her new room.

The street light shining through the window made friendly patterns on the floor.

In the morning she said to her brother, "There is
something hiding under my bed. It doesn't make a sound
till the lights are out. Then it huffs a little and slides on
the floor in the dark. But it will never come out. It's
afraid of floating."

Her brother came to look under the bed with his
flashlight. "It's only dust," he said.

Jenny didn't even look.

Jenny found a matchbox under the hall radiator. She knew that something lived inside. It probably looked like a pumpkin seed, but it had a tiny fierce roar and a little tail that swished and swashed.

Jenny didn't tell anyone about it — not her mother or her father or her brother. She just put the matchbox under her pillow where it would be perfectly safe.

At night in the quiet new house, Jenny listened. From beneath her pillow came a humming roar, so soft, so very soft, that no one else could possibly hear it.

Jenny fell asleep.